P R

MW01015517

Top 10 Romance of 2012, 2015, and 2016.

— BOOKLIST: THE NIGHT IS MINE, HOT
POINT, HEART STRIKE

One of our favorite authors.

— RT BOOK REVIEWS

Buchman has catapulted his way to the top tier of my favorite authors.

— FRESH FICTION

A favorite author of mine. I'll read anything that carries his name, no questions asked. Meet your new favorite author!

— THE SASSY BOOKSTER, FLASH OF
FIRE

M.L. Buchman is guaranteed to get me lost in a good story.

— THE READING CAFE, WAY OF THE
WARRIOR: NSDQ

I love Buchman's writing. His vivid descriptions bring everything to life in an unforgettable way.

— PURE JONEL, HOT POINT

#3   3-10-18

WHEN THEY JUST KNOW

AN OREGON FIREBIRDS ROMANCE

M. L. BUCHMAN

Buchman Bookworks

SIGN UP FOR M. L. BUCHMAN'S
NEWSLETTER TODAY

and receive:
Release News
Free Short Stories
a Free book

Do it today. Do it now.
http://free-book.mlbuchman.com

Other works by M. L. Buchman:

*J*ana Williams sat on a lawn chair beside the Denali pickup, clicking her hooks together while staring at the smoke-gray sky. She should be doing paperwork, checking bank balances (always a serious worry, though not as bad as at the start of their first-ever firefighting season), following the feeds from the six MD 520N firefighting helicopters that made up the Firebirds team…something constructive.

Instead, she was parked in the summer- and wind-parched landscape of Oregon's Columbia River Gorge beneath a smoke-stained, dark Purgatory of a sky, while wildfire threatened the farms around Hood River. The tarmac of Ken Jernstedt Airfield shimmered with the summer heat, hazing the tied-down small airplanes almost to invisibility though they were only a few hundred meters away.

And the most useful thing she could think to do was clicking her hooks.

It had started as an innocuous habit.

Back before she'd lost her right hand, she'd had a habit

of fooling with her hair when she was worrying at a problem. She'd found a much-needed distraction in the tactile slickness as it ran through her fingers, so smooth and fine that it almost didn't feel as if it was there at all. It was like playing with golden water. She'd wind it around her fingers one way, then the other. And while some portion of her mind and body had been distracted doing that, she'd been able to think.

Thinking seemed to come much harder now.

After the accident and the end of her Army career, she still had the habit. But her hair snagged painfully in the mechanism of the hooks. Left-handed hair fiddling hadn't been nearly as satisfying. Besides, that hand was now twice as busy as ever because it had to do most of the work of both hands. If she was going to lose a hand, why couldn't it have been the left one? It still took her forever to sign a distorted version of her name, and fancy stuff like tying shoelaces, just totally sucked.

It was even worse when, like now, she was worrying at a problem but didn't even know what it was.

Now she really needed some right-handed distraction, as if her phantom hand was still sending encrypted orders after the dropped Hellfire missile had crushed it past recovery. She supposed that she should feel lucky that the missile hadn't exploded when the arms tech had misfastened the mount on her Sikorsky MH-60 Blackhawk. Jana had wiggled it during a preflight check of her aircraft —and it had let go.

Had her hand made the difference in easing the impact of the hundred-pound missile hitting the steel deck of the aircraft carrier? Had she averted disaster or just pointlessly sacrificed her hand? No one could say for sure. The stupid medal they gave her as a replacement for her hand certainly didn't answer the question.

On her more cynical days—she tried not to think of them as morose or, god forbid, depressed—she'd wonder if she'd have been better off letting the damn thing fall and explode. Instead, she was left to appease her phantom hand and wonder.

Clicking her hooks together had taken some practice. She had to extend her arm to increase the distance between the hooks and where the harness anchored in a strap that ran behind her back and around to her left shoulder. She could also hunch her left shoulder forward. Either technique would stretch the distance and open the hooks; shrink it and the rubber band at the hooks' base pulled them back together. Her innocent finger-twirl had turned into a shoulder twitch.

Jana often debated whether it would be more or less satisfying if her hooks didn't have rubber gripper pads on the insides. It was more of a soft tap than a satisfying metallic click. Maybe…

Maybe she was totally coming apart. No real question about that actually.

"Nice to just stop for a minute," Maggie Torres, the Firebirds miracle helicopter mechanic, plummeted into the chair beside her. She handed over a bottle of water still slick with condensation before opening her own.

Jana appreciated that Maggie never tried to second guess or help. They'd had a discussion of what Jana could and couldn't do with her hooks, and Maggie had never forgotten once. Whether it was Maggie-the-mechanic or Maggie-the-friend who remembered, Jana didn't ask. Friends had always been a tricky thing for her and she didn't like to question what few tenuous ties she had to the world of fully configured humans.

Jana stretched her right elbow out and down and could feel the tension on her left shoulder as the harness took up the slack. She spread the hooks over the bottle's plastic top, then eased the tension. The hooks clamped down hard. With a sharp twist of her left hand, she got it unscrewed.

The chill water felt good sliding down her raw throat. The summer's late afternoon heat, the smoky air, and feeling like shit had left her throat achingly dry.

"How's the crew?"

Jana shrugged, one shoulder, because two would open her hooks and she'd have to fish the bottle cap out of the scrub grass. Instead, she waved her hooks at the radio she'd propped up on the pickup's bumper. That motion made her drop the cap anyway. She ignored it. Just as she'd been ignoring the radio.

They both listened for a moment.

"Sounds like normal flight operations to me," Maggie surmised.

Jana had to agree. Today's mission for the Firebirds was saving farms: house, barn, and livestock—any orchards were an optional bonus. After half a season together, it was easy to pick out the team's voices. Though one of them always sounded strange to her ears.

Jasper Abrams, her brother's best friend, never spoke in camp, only in the air. Occasionally he would grunt at her brother—who led the Firebirds even if his wife Stacy was a better pilot. But that was about all Jasper ever did on the ground and even that was rare.

Whereas in the air—

"*H*ey! You *can* hit the side of a barn." Jasper slid in close, flying his helo in the Number Two slot behind Curt's.

He was also close enough to see the results of the unexpected downdraft over the barn. The faded red barn was an old-style high-peaked roof with a hayloft above and cattle below. The fire-driven wind scooted fast over the top of the tall structure and created a Venturi effect turbulence wake on the backside of the barn. Curt's load of water had been dumped, and then been sucked into the low pressure zone. Rather than dousing the encroaching fire, it had washed fifty years of grime off the side of the barn.

"Of course you can't hit the fire to save your life." Now that Curt's drop had revealed the effect, Jasper was able to anticipate and use it. He dumped his two hundred gallons a second later than instinct said to. As he flew away, he twisted the helo sideways so that he could see the results. The fifteen-hundred pounds of water was sucked in by the backdraft and slammed into the fire with a perfect drop.

Amos whooped out a cheer as he blasted the rest of

the fire into the ground. One more pass by the three of them to make sure the fire traveled around the barn and not through it—then they could move on to the neighbor's. After that there was a long bend in the Columbia River that would serve as a firebreak for the fire to die against.

The late afternoon light was lost in long loops of the smoky sky. This fire wasn't big enough to call the heavy teams off the burn out near Spokane, Washington. It was Firebirds sized.

"Show us the way, oh fearless leader," Jasper twisted back into line behind Curt. He wasn't sure why he was in such a good mood. It wasn't often that Curt messed up even a little, and he liked getting a dig in on him. They'd been toe-and-heel since elementary school. Their rivalry had always been evenly matched—in the air and on the ground.

Until now.

Curt had found the woman of his dreams. Stacy Richardson certainly flew and looked like one. He wasn't envious—Stacy wasn't really his type even if she was Curt's. It was part of what had always worked between them. There'd only been a couple times that they'd ever gunned for the same girl...but Jasper's heart had never really been in it when they did overlap.

The golden hills of Washington leaned down over the Columbia as they flew over to retank their helicopters. The light brown of dry summer grasses and the green swatches of conifers so dark that they looked black against the grass. The river itself flowed slow and wide.

To the south the towering peak of Mount Hood was mostly obscured, the glaring white glaciers only peeking through at opportune moments like a white firebrand in the sky.

For Jasper there'd always been one girl who overshadowed them all.

But fourteen-year-olds didn't get to go out with their best friend's eighteen-year-old sister. By the time he was finally out of high school, she was leaving college and headed straight into the Army. His and Curt's graduation had been the same day as Jana's, so there hadn't even been a road trip from Portland, Oregon down to UC Berkeley. She'd gone straight from graduation to Fort Rucker, Alabama as an Aviation Officer.

The woman who'd come home on leave had been almost unrecognizable and had left him beyond his normal tongue-tied. Her long blonde hair chopped jawline short and her cross-country runner body turned powerful and sculpted. She'd also had an equally chiseled aviator boyfriend in tow that had almost killed him to see.

And if Jasper didn't pay attention, he was going to fly straight into Curt's rotors and kill them both for real.

He slid thirty meters to the side and descended to a low hover over the Columbia River. The water here flowed deep and smooth, reflecting their helicopters off its glassy dark blue.

He dropped the snorkel hose into the water and kicked on the pumps. He kept one eye on the gauge as he sucked up two hundred gallons into the helo's belly tank in twenty seconds. He kept the other eye on the lazily flowing river, slowly adding lift to maintain his altitude as he added sixteen-hundred pounds to a helicopter that weighed only that much when empty.

Amos settled beyond him so that they hovered in a long line over the river.

Curt was up and away well before Jasper due to his momentary fumble.

Did Jana have to be so damned distracting?

She'd come back from the Army a broken woman. He knew the loss of her hand ate at her. But losing her career and the Dear Jana from her fiancé—which made him both thrilled and have a serious desire to bust the guy's balls for deserting her—had really thrown her for a loop.

For lack of anywhere else to be, she'd taken to staying at Curt's while they flew firefighting for Columbia helicopters. She'd started to look like she was going to rot in place as she went quietly stir crazy.

He'd joined and eventually captained the high school cross-country running team just as Jana had four years ahead of him. And when he remembered that, he'd shown up at Curt's apartment one day and tossed her running shoes at her.

"Let's go," were the first words he'd said directly to her since his highly lucid, "Oh, man!" when she came home with one less hand than she'd left with.

She'd glared at him from the couch. One-handed or not, she was still the most amazing woman he'd ever seen. She'd finally barked out a sharp, "Fine!" and put on the shoes. Her balance was an issue for the first mile or so. After that, they just ran. Every day before he left for work. She even started coming out to the fireline. They never spoke, but they ran together almost every morning for the last three years. It was a strange relationship, but it was the best one he'd ever had.

Then when her and Curt's parents had died, it had taken everything just to survive that. They'd been second parents to him, but his best friend and Jana had barely made it through. But they had, and now they flew.

He, Curt, and Amos doused the last of the fire at the barn and were soon chasing the flames as they started on the neighbor's apple orchard. Here, each tree saved was precious. No swatch of annual wheat, but living tree with plenty of years to bear fruit.

Amos and Curt were still ragging each other about something.

But all Jasper could think was how Jana had looked during this morning's run. Her hair was again long, just over her shoulders—the color of sunshine. She ran in gym shorts and a tight t-shirt. Rather than a fire shirt, honoring whatever wildfire they'd recently flown to, it was a helicopter shirt—*Helicopters don't fly, they beat the air into submission.* That described Jana perfectly.

She knocked the breath out of him every single time he looked at her.

A fact he'd never told anyone. Especially not his best friend.

"Let's bring it home, buddy."

"Yep!" Jasper did his best to join in. "We beat that one into submission." And they had. The fire hadn't gotten anywhere near the last barn. They'd even saved a significant portion of his fruit orchard.

"Got a hot lady waiting for me." Curt always had to rub it in.

"Asshole!" Twelve of the last thirteen hours had been in the air. The idea that he was going back to his woman had Curt supercharged despite the hard day. Jasper was going to creak when he climbed down.

"Stacy's got you so whipped, my friend." Curt's wife had him completely wrapped around her pinkie.

"Absolutely!" Curt took full ownership of the slur.

What was Jasper supposed to do with someone that ridiculously pleased with his life?

"I got Stacy. Palo got Maggie. My new mission is getting you a hot babe."

"Me, too," Amos called over the radio.

"What?" Jasper could deal with Amos. "We all thought you and Drew were like forever-after-together dudes." The two of them joked and bickered like twins, even during babe-reconnaissance at the local pub.

Amos could only sputter in protest.

Jasper didn't need some hot babe. He had a woman waiting…

Except she didn't know it and it was becoming clear that he was never going to tell her. Because as long as he never asked, the answer would never be "Hell no!" He didn't think his ego could take that. And he'd rather be part of Jana's life and never have her, than not be around her at all.

*J*ana waited as the first three helos returned from the firefight to land on the tarmac at Jernstedt field. Stacy landed first, with Palo and Drew hot on her heels, because none of the pilots could keep up with Stacy. At each helo, Jana would plug in her tablet computer and download all of the flight data and video. The Firebirds were partially financed by the insurance companies for all of the structures they saved and this documentation was their income in a very real way.

She ignored the pain of even touching a helicopter each time, trying to accept that she couldn't fly it. Why couldn't she have lost a foot? Feet were simple. All they had to do was push on a rudder pedal. But without a hand, the complexities of the multiple controls on the head of the cyclic joystick were beyond her capacity.

The ache in her heart was good though. It reminded her that she was alive. Like the ache in her body when she ran each day with Jasper.

He'd saved her life with that running. She hadn't been

in complete despair yet, but she'd been able to feel the end lurking off in the distance. Unable to do the only thing she'd ever loved—to fly—what was left for her? And Jasper had reminded her of something she'd forgotten: the simple joy of running.

For a long time that daily run was her lifeline. It was almost an illness when they missed a day. She never ran alone. Even though he never spoke to her, it had felt disloyal to run without him. It was stupid, she knew, but it was Jasper who had reconnected her to…herself.

Whoever the hell that was.

Maggie rushed up to Palo's helo the moment the engine cycled down and practically threw herself into the cockpit.

Stacy looked up at the sky as she stretched out the kinks of a long day aloft.

"He's five minutes out," Jana told her as she plugged her tablet into Stacy's helo.

Her new sister-in-law flashed a smile at her. "Am I that obvious?"

"Yes."

Stacy laughed. "I'm just so happy. I keep waiting to wake up."

"Don't," Jana actually gave Stacy a one-armed hug that surprised them both. She stepped aside quickly.

"I can't thank you enough times for hiring me."

"Or for letting you have my little brother. I know, you keep telling me," which came out kinda crappy—which was more about her pain-in-the-neck little brother than Stacy. "You're welcome to him," which didn't sound much better.

Stacy was eyeing her like she was a grenade that might or might not still have a pin in it.

"Seriously, Stacy. I've never seen Curt happier than

when he's with you. Let's call it sisterly jealousy and leave it at that."

"Okay, Jana." It was a stiff response by Stacy standards who had every bit of naturally bubbly that Jana had never been able to cultivate.

"Shit! I'm being a crappy sister-in-law." She unplugged her tablet from the helo and prepared to move on.

"Jana," Stacy stopped her with a hand on her good arm. Stacy looked right at her with those big brown eyes of hers that had sucked her brother right in. "You're my idol —you know that, right? *You* are the woman I keep trying to be."

Jana's jaw didn't go loose, but it felt as if it should. She had no idea what to say to that except perhaps recommend her sister-in-law get some serious counseling.

"You're so strong. I know my husband's shortcomings. I guess they're part of what I love about him. I know that *you* are the one who built the Firebirds. I'd never have thought to do something like that."

"I didn't think it up, he did."

"Really? Curt? That doesn't sound like him at all."

And she was right. Curt was a straight-ahead guy's guy. A good and patient leader, but not one for thinking outside of the box. He was in charge because he was the kind of guy that people flocked to and stuck with. She'd only ever achieved that by being a better pilot than everyone around her. When Curt had met Stacy, a pilot better than he was, he hadn't competed with her—he'd married her.

The second half of the Firebirds entered the airfield's pattern and swooped down the runway before carving a final turn into the section of the airfield allocated for their use. Even though the fire was beaten, the upper atmosphere was still thick with dust and smoke. They were definitely getting "red at night." It wasn't even sunset and the sky was bloody.

She and Stacy stood together and watched them land and shut down. No need to glance at the tail number to see who flew which of the otherwise identical birds.

Amos rushed to be first on the ground. The instant he was down, he and his best pal Drew would be off to the motel to clean up. The rest of the crew would catch up with them at the pub where they'd be chatting up women with easy success.

Curt did his usual straightforward: fly here, land there.

Jasper flew the way he ran—dead smooth, stretching out those long legs of his to eat up the distance. Everything about him integrated into a single motion.

Smooth even as he climbed out of the cockpit and pulled on his ridiculous trademark cowboy hat—as if a man who stood six-foot-three had a height inferiority complex.

"You know that your family left Texas when you were four."

"Six." It had become their standard greeting—never anything more. This time was no exception.

His family had moved in next door. Six-year-old Curt had been instantly enamored of Jasper's cool hat. He'd been at that cowboys-are-cool age.

At ten, Jana had been too self-conscious and sophisticated a girl to deign to notice him beyond trying to be nice to their new neighbor—mostly because it got her little brother out of her hair.

Jasper had lived in the thing then just as he did now. He wore it every day, even when they went running. No amount of razzing in school had deterred him. Jana had learned a lot from watching a much younger Jasper stand by the firm conviction of his beliefs. He'd made her wonder what *she* believed in.

And now? Without the Army, without her hand, the only thing she believed in was the Firebirds. It was enough to keep her sane, marginally. *One day at a time, Jana.* Her mantra ever since she'd woken up without her hand.

Jasper continued to loom above her.

Curt and Stacy were busy doing their newlywed greeting thing.

She wished they'd wait until they were back in their room—or another state. It was petty of her, but all their antics did was make her that much more uncomfortable two steps from the silent Jasper.

"I'll just get your data," she stepped around Jasper who wasn't moving.

He nodded his hat, his dark eyes almost invisible beneath the brim.

She'd only made it two more steps past him when Stacy called out.

"Hey, Jana. Curt says that the Firebirds was actually Jasper's idea."

Curt nodded as Jana's gaze swept over him on her way to face Jasper.

Jasper remained frozen in place with his back to her for several seconds. Then he turned slowly to face her.

"But he never said a word. Not in all that planning." She'd given up addressing him directly as he never spoke to her—directly *or* indirectly.

"No," Curt stepped over. "He had it all hashed out when he ran it by me over beers one night. You know, I've been meaning to ask you since forever, Jasper, what the hell do you have against my sister?"

Jasper didn't turn to Curt, but continued to look right at her.

She wanted to fool with her hair, or click her hooks, or something, but instead remained in a frozen stillness waiting for the answer. It didn't feel like hate, but he certainly never spoke to her.

"It goes back since I can remember," Curt never did know when to keep his mouth shut. "Did she piss on your cowboy hat the day you moved in or something?"

"Nope," Jasper answered Curt without looking away from her.

"Then what? I mean—" Curt jolted like he'd been pinched. "What?" he turned on Stacy. So Stacy had pinched him.

Go, girl!

She just rolled her eyes at him. "Come along, dear." And she towed a bewildered Curt away, leaving her alone with Jasper.

Something in his look kept Jana's voice stuck in her throat.

The fuel truck's diesel engine thudded by them as the tanker moved in to refuel the helos. The on-board pump ground to life as the service tech started down the line pumping out Jet A gas. The sharp bite of kerosene accented the wood smoke still hovering in the air.

"I thought up the Firebirds for you after your parents died," Jasper finally spoke to her. It felt as if it was the first time in years. His voice was low and soft. Impossible to disbelieve. Impossible to ignore. The loss of her parents had been a gut shot to them all. It had sent her spiraling down all over again.

"For me?" She managed.

He nodded his head, which was much more about his hat.

"Like the running after the Army," which had gotten her out of the darkest place she'd ever been.

16

Again the nod.

"Your idea was that poor Jana needed therapy, so you provided it?" Her voice was rising now.

Enough that the fuel truck driver was looking her direction.

"No. I—"

"Poor crippled Jana needs some asshole to take care of her because she can't take care of herself anymore!" Rather than going louder, she felt her voice go low and nasty…and she couldn't stop it. "Well, I don't need anybody. And I sure don't need you, Jasper Jones."

He remained unmoving throughout her tirade.

The words were out there and she could never take them back.

To hell with the last three helos' data.

To hell with the money that data represented.

To hell with her brother and his ever-so-happy life.

"To hell with you, Jasper Jones."

If she hadn't cried when she lost her hand, she sure as hell wasn't going to cry now.

Instead she turned away.

Helo in front of her.

Get in! Fly away! Now!

She placed a foot on the small steel pad on one of the skid's legs. Got her other foot up and into the cockpit.

That's when six years of habit flying the Black Hawks betrayed her.

She reached out with her right hand to grab the handhold and pull her upper body in.

Except she no longer had a right hand.

*J*asper watched her go. The words he'd feared since the day he'd first spotted the sun-blonde girl next door had finally happened. The only door he really cared about other than Curt's friendship had just been slammed in his face.

He hung his head so that his hat blocked out any view of Jana walking away from him. If only he could have—

A startled cry had him looking up again quickly. Jana had climbed halfway into the helicopter.

Her right arm flailed as she fell backward. He looked up in time to see her try to save herself by grabbing the edge of the doorframe with her good hand, but momentum ripped her fingers free.

He took one step. Two…

But he was too late, Jana went down hard. Her metal hooks made a sharp grinding as they skidding across the pavement when she tried to stave off the fall. Her head hit with a sickening thud. She groaned once and, going limp, lay still.

"Shit!" Jasper dropped to his knees beside her, but

didn't know what to do. "Curt! Anyone!" He screamed the last, but couldn't look up.

He reached for her twice, but couldn't complete the gesture. Then he remembered his basic CPR training.

No sign of blood spreading over the pavement. Check.

Breathing? He noted the rise and fall of her chest through the thin t-shirt she wore. Definitely breathing. Check. *Now look the hell away, man!*

He reached for her wrist...but it was made of plastic. Her flesh arm was twisted behind her back, though the angle didn't look weird or anything.

Jasper rested his hand on the curve over her throat. Not how he'd pictured their first ever touch. Jana's skin was incredibly smooth and soft. He felt the first beat of her pulse when someone suddenly knelt on Jana's other side.

Then a fist plowed into Jasper's jaw.

It was a good hit and sent him flying backward.

"What the hell did you do to her?" Curt screamed at him. "Why have you always hated her so much?"

He opened his mouth, but his jaw hurt like hell.

"You're an idiot, Curt," Stacy spoke up for him. "He doesn't hate Jana. He loves her."

He thought only *he* knew. He'd guarded the secret for so long that he couldn't answer now that it was out in the world. Now he could only close his eyes and bow his head.

He did love Jana. And didn't that just totally suck for him.

*J*ana woke slowly with her head nestled cozily in someone's lap. It was warm there. Safe.

The roar of a diesel engine was distant. Muted.

A cool hand rested for a moment on her forehead. She didn't remember taking a lover to bed last night. She hadn't taken one in a long, long time that she could recall.

There was a hard jostle, enough to make her head explode with pain. She might not see stars, but she felt as if she'd been hit by a nebula, maybe an entire galaxy.

"Shh, Jana. We're almost there."

She risked opening one eye and squinted up at Stacy's breasts. A slight shift of focus and she saw her face looking down worriedly.

"Where…" was all she managed in a dry croak.

"Back of one of our pickup trucks. Almost to the hospital."

"You're not driving," Jana could hear the racing engine. Stacy was notorious as the only member on the team who always drove exactly on the speed limit.

"Maggie is. We wanted to get you there this century," Stacy half smiled and then smoothed her hand over Jana's forehead again.

"Wha—"

Maggie must have jumped a curb the size of an aircraft hangar—the jumbo jet size. Her world exploded in a flash of white pain.

"Easy, Maggie," Stacy called out loudly enough to make Jana cringe.

She tried to cover her ears. One side worked. On the other side all she did was ram her hooks into Stacy's side.

"Hey!" Stacy grunted out.

"Sorry. Pothole," Maggie called from the front. "They grow them big around here."

"What hap—" Jana tried again but could only squeeze her eyes tight as they slewed around a corner like a banking Sikorsky Black Hawk under heavy fire.

"Missed that one," Maggie called out happily.

"We're not sure," Stacy was looking down at her steadily, as if the truck wasn't on an insane roller coaster ride.

"You were talking to Jasper when I turned my back. Next thing I know you're flat on the ground and Jasper is kneeling over you freaking out and crying for help. He said you ran into a helicopter."

She'd run into something. Hard. She'd been too… something to see what it was. All Jana remembered was the helpless flail as both her hand and her hooks failed her. She'd—they slammed over another bump.

"That one *was* a curb. Sorry," Maggie spoke up.

Jana remembered losing her balance, but that was the last thing. "Must have fallen and knocked myself out."

"By the size of the lump on your head, we were

thinking that you ran at the helo headfirst with all your might."

"Lump?" She reached for it.

"Hey! Hey! Cut that out," there was a pressure on her arm. Stacy was fending off Jana's right arm and hooks.

"Sorry," she tried again with the left and couldn't stop the hiss of pain when she found the bump. "Oh my god. That's huge!"

"Hence the race to the hospital."

"And…we're here!" Maggie slammed on the big truck's brakes hard enough to chirp the tires and almost enough to tumble Jana out of Stacy's lap and onto the backseat's floor.

Jana tried to sit up, but Stacy used that cool hand on her forehead to keep her in place.

"Don't you dare. Now lie still. You sit up and puke all over this truck, we're going to leave it for you to clean up. You puke on me and you might have to find yourself a new sister-in-law."

"Okay, Stacy."

And she lay there, oddly at peace with her head in Stacy's lap. Being taken care of. It wasn't something she was used to, but Stacy's inner kindness made it easy to accept.

Taken care of.

She'd been protesting about just that to someone recently.

Telling someone…no, *yelling* at someone that she didn't need that. This. But she liked this.

The door next to Stacy opened and a pair of blue-gloved hands held either side of her head as Stacy slid out. Then they placed a board beneath her before they eased her out the door and onto a rolling gurney.

"All I did was bump my head." Then her head hit the

soft pillow and she yelped. One side might be soft, but someone must have hidden a brick under the other side.

"Easy," the blue-gloved doctor said. "I don't want to turn your head until we've checked out there are no neck injuries."

Jana was good with that. More than once she'd seen a helo pilot coming off a crash landing with a broken back. Please don't let her have that now. Please not that too.

So she lay on the gurney keeping her thoughts to herself as they slid a strap over her forehead and another across her shoulders. She missed Stacy's cool hand.

That's when she remembered why she'd run into the helicopter.

She'd been yelling at…Jasper.

Jana closed her eyes and groaned.

"How badly does it hurt?" Stacy asked as she crushed Jana's one hand in both of hers.

It hurt bad. The things she'd said to Jasper…

Why couldn't she have kept *those* thoughts to herself?

6

"*N*uh-uh. I know that look."

"What look?" Jasper couldn't turn to face Curt. All he could see was the cloud of dust Maggie had left as she'd raced away toward the hospital.

"That I'm-going-to-leave-and-never-come-back look. I saw Palo try that on Maggie. I get it now."

Palo spoke up from his other side, "Don't do it, bro. The payoff ain't there. I'm telling you."

Jasper watched the dust that refused to settle in the baking twilit air. Everything was smudged and dirty. His hands from working over a fire all day. The sky. All of his dreams.

"I'm not gonna let you," Curt was still on old news.

Jasper turned to Palo. "Where is the payoff then?"

"Hitting the homerun," Curt could be a peacock strutting his shit. Now he and Palo both ignored him.

Jasper waited while Palo chewed on his answer. Curt finally caught on and kept his yap shut until Palo was ready to speak.

"Don't take 'no' for an answer," he finally offered.

"It was a mighty thorough, in-my-face 'no' to be ignoring."

"Then man up!" Curt's answer to almost everything, but Palo nodded his agreement. Curt and Stacy had been such an obvious fit from the first moment, that it seemed there'd been no other possibility. Palo'd had his work cut out for him to win Maggie's heart, yet he'd pulled it off. Maybe Jasper should trust him.

He pulled out his keys and headed for his Camaro.

"Oh no you don't!" Curt grabbed his arm.

Jasper's jaw still hurt like hell and he could feel the pressure of the swelling around his eye. He considered returning the favor, but couldn't think of any reason to do so. Curt had just been defending Jana, something Jasper had been trying to do his entire life.

Jasper yanked his arm free. "I'm going to the hospital to check on her. That's all."

"Then I'm coming with you."

"Fine."

"Fine?" Curt clearly didn't believe him. Not that Jasper cared. As long as Curt didn't remember what Stacy had said about Jasper's true feelings. How the hell had she known anyway?

"Fine. Get in the car," and Jasper climbed into his black-and-flame painted Camaro. He looked back at Palo, "You coming?"

Palo shook his head. "Maggie would kill me if I left with her helos unsecured."

Jasper nodded. The man knew his woman. Then he and Curt rolled out the front gate and headed for the hospital which lay just four miles away through town.

Curt let the first three-point-eight go by in silence, then asked, "Since when have you loved Jana?"

Jasper focused on the last two-tenths as he rolled into

the hospital parking lot and found a spot close by the Firebirds' big, black Denali pickup. Jasper closed his eyes and leaned back in his seat, keeping his hands on the wheel.

"Well?"

He sighed, but finally answered. "Since the first moment I saw her."

"You were six."

"So were you."

"Sis was ten."

"She was."

Curt started to laugh.

Jasper glared over at him.

"Got a thing for older women, do you?"

Jasper debated if it was enough reason to hit his best friend—at least a knuckle punch on the nerve center in his upper arm. But he couldn't find the motivation.

"Only since I was six," he got out of the car and went to find Jana.

7

"*We*'re keeping you overnight," the civilian doctor actually tried to sound soothing which was better than most Army docs managed. "Gave yourself a hell of a whack there and a moderate concussion."

Not being a stupid doctor, he also retreated before Jana could manage more than a feeble protest. They'd given her a prescription strength Tylenol, but it didn't seem to be doing anything for the steady thud of the headache emanating from the lump on the back of her head.

Maggie and Stacy came up to either side of her bed the moment the doctor cleared out.

"It sounds good," Stacy had been hanging out with her brother too much. She had become almost as matter-of-fact as Curt. Or had she been that way from the beginning?

"Good?" Jana protested.

"You aren't dead, honey," Maggie brushed Jana's hair away from her face.

"A blessing of small favors," she closed her eyes. She

was glad she was mostly uninjured. The only part of her that she wished was dead at the moment was the part that had told Jasper to go to hell for being nice to her.

"What?" Stacy took her hand and held it. That made her aware that her other hand had been removed and was sitting on the side table. It took her a couple of tries, and some embarrassing help from Maggie, to get her stump out of sight beneath the sheet. Even that grated at her, though it was a simple kindness. Had she so isolated herself from everyone?

"I said awful things to Jasper. Things he didn't deserve. At least I don't think so. It's all muddled up. Anyway, I totally screwed up everything, as usual."

"You're not the only one," Stacy's voice was laced with enough chagrin to make Jana open her eyes once more. Stacy seemed to take a sudden interest in a heart monitor that wasn't showing anything, because the doctor hadn't turned it on. The only sound in the room was the air conditioning and the quiet chatter of a couple nurses at their station down the hall.

"Spill it."

"Uh…"

Jana risked moving her head to check on Maggie, but she was watching Stacy with wide eyes. Curiosity…or not believing that Stacy was about to reveal some dark secret? Jana couldn't tell.

"Stacy?"

"I…might have…said something. Something that maybe I shouldn't."

"What? To who?"

"To Curt."

"What did you say to my brother?"

"That…" Now Stacy was taking an interest in the ceiling tiles. When she went to step away, Jana held her

30

hand tighter, even giving it a slight yank to make Stacy look at her. The gesture was a mistake, as at the moment everything in her body seemed to be connected to the throbbing lump on the back of her head.

"Stacy…"

Stacy blushed bright pink to the ears.

"I said—"

"There she is! Hey, Sis," Curt's voice boomed into the room, almost splitting Jana's head in two.

She winced until the pressure wave of the sound blast stopped echoing inside her head. When her eyes were able to refocus, she saw that someone was hiding behind Curt.

It wasn't working.

Her brother might be six-foot tall and have broad shoulders that Stacy couldn't help gushing about. But the lean man hiding behind him was six-foot-three and was topped by another several inches of cowboy hat.

"Get out!" Now her own voice was hurting her head.

The visible part of the cowboy hat turned for the door.

"No! Not you, Jasper. Everyone else, out. Now."

"But…" Stacy held onto her hand.

Jana squeezed it briefly, then let go. "Shoo," she whispered it softly.

"Buddy!" Curt slapped Jasper on the shoulder hard enough to send him stumbling into a wall. He turned to Jana, "You wouldn't believe what he said about—"

Jasper grabbed him by the wrist, flipped it up behind Curt's back hard enough to make him squeak in pain, before Jasper shoved him out the door hard enough that he almost hit the wall on the other side of the hall.

It took some cajoling to get the women to leave. Enough that Jana was beginning to wonder just how blind she'd been about Maggie's and Stacy's loyalty to her. They kept trying to hover, even when she didn't want them to.

She apparently had real friends, despite how she brushed people off.

Stacy patted Jasper on the shoulder as she left. Maggie, who was over a foot shorter, pulled him down to kiss him on the cheek.

As the room cleared, she wondered how in the world she was going to take back the things she'd said to Jasper. She'd meant…some of it. But not all. She could feel a whirling mix of fear that Jasper would decide to leave the Firebirds and joy that he was here in her hospital room. The two combined to leave her feeling rather nauseated despite the drugs the doctor had given her for just that.

At last it was just them, though she could hear the others clustered outside the door having a whispered conversation.

At her signal, Jasper closed the door.

"Jasper, I…" No, she was being a coward, staring at the white ceiling. She turned to look directly at him. "Jasper, I… What the hell happened to your face?" One cheek and eye were purpling badly and the eye was half swollen shut.

"Your brother," he spoke barely above a mumble.

"Curt punched you?"

"I suppose that for a moment he thought I was the one who'd knocked you out. He's even more protective of you than I am. You hit the ground hard. Scared me halfway back to Texas. Guess you scared him worse and he saw me kneeling over you with my hand at your throat."

"At my throat?" Jana swallowed her throat suddenly felt dry.

"I was trying to make sure you had a pulse."

"A pulse?"

Jasper nodded.

"And that prompted the longest sentence you've ever spoken to me."

Jasper shrugged.

"Why do you hate me so much?"

"I don't."

And he was right. A man who hated her wouldn't rescue her by taking her out running. A man who hated her wouldn't think up something as elegant as the Firebirds to give her a purpose when her parents were gone and she'd needed one so desperately.

"Okay…" She thought about it a minute. "Then why don't you ever speak to me?"

8

"*B*ecause I..." Jasper desperately wanted to admit to being an idiot and then walk away while he still could. But that sounded even lamer than the truth.

Jana waited for him.

To buy himself a moment, he poured her a paper cup of water from a small carafe. But there was no straw for her to drink it while she was lying down, so he drank it himself. Then tried to figure out what to do with the little cup. Not the sharps bin. Not...

He set it on the white steel table by the carafe and her disconnected arm. It was strange seeing the hooks without her attached.

Forcing himself, he turned to her. By her perfect stillness it was obvious how much she was hurting. He could also see by the lines of the thin white sheet that she wore nothing other than an even thinner hospital gown beneath that. There was an extra bit of flatness along her right side where the hooks should be.

Over the years he'd seen Jana looking elegant in a prom dress or hot in a swimsuit—thankfully she'd favored

35

one-pieces over bikinis or it might have killed him. In full military dress, she'd been imposing. In casual camp gear, she'd been a treat.

But lying here, he was forced to take a step closer.

"Is it hard being back in a hospital?"

Her darting look away told him just how hard. She actually shivered.

He took the blanket from the foot of her bed and spread it over her. He pulled up a chair by her bedside and waited her out.

She finally nodded, but still didn't look at him.

"I'm sorry I made you so angry."

"Maybe…I shouldn't have been," she stayed focused on the far wall.

"Would it have helped if I'd told you the things I was planning back when I was planning them?"

"Duh," and she moved enough to stare at the white fluorescent ceiling fixture for a while. At length, she finally looked at him. "Though to be honest, maybe not. If you'd told me you were taking me out running because I was busy making myself even more depressed with each passing day, I might have force fed you my sneakers."

"And the Firebirds?"

"I don't know. It was so elegant. It saved me. It saved both of us. It got Curt in charge of his own company, which he always wanted. It got him Stacy which is a gift beyond any he ever dreamed of."

Jasper knew that. He'd seen his best friend come to life from the moment they met. He knew what that felt like, deep inside. Every time Jana brushed against his life—even just a quick overseas text to Curt that was mentioned in passing—had breathed life into him.

"If you'd told me, would I have believed in it any less?

Would I have worked any less hard to make it happen? I don't know."

"You liked that it was for your family. For you and Curt."

"I did," Jana nodded, with only a small wince of pain this time.

Jasper had known that about her. However much she'd complained about her little brother while they were growing up, the love was there like a shining streak of sunlight.

"I'd lost all hope after I did this," she raised her right arm and it slipped clear of the sheets. "You found a way to give that back to me."

He'd never seen her stump before. Jana Williams was *never* in public without her arm on. Even in the early days, when he knew it was hurting her, she wouldn't take it off.

He'd almost expected something hideous with how she hid it so carefully. But it looked as natural as could be. He couldn't even see any scars at the end. Her arm simply tapered to a stubby point, a little wider than the bone that still remained within.

She saw where he was looking and tried to tuck it back out of sight.

Before she could, he simply lay his hand on the remaining upper part of her forearm, to show her it was okay.

9

*J*ana's breath caught in her throat.

No one touched her arm. The last person had been an Army physical therapist three years ago.

But Jasper's hand lay upon her skin as calmly as if it was the most normal thing in the world. She could feel herself switch from frozen stiff to blind panic.

"Easy, Jana. Just breathe. Okay? Just breathe."

And somehow, his hand, lying so casually upon her hideous stub, let her do that. Let her breathe.

Jasper sighed. "The reason I don't talk to you?"

She nodded, welcoming any distraction. His fingers began tracing lightly over her skin. Small movements, so tiny they probably weren't conscious. But they stroked the skin by her elbow as if it was just…skin. Such a strange feeling.

"You were always so out of reach. Too old when I was kid. Then married to your job and engaged to Captain What's His Name."

Captain What's His Name had never been her fiancé.

He was gay as could be. But they'd become super close friends. She'd been his excuse to avoid the harassment that still existed in so many places, including his own family so he'd taken his leaves with her instead of going home. He'd been her shield against unwelcome advances. He'd kept promising to come visit her—she was the one who'd told him no and shut him out. Apparently he had also been a signal to Jasper to steer clear.

"Once you were injured and he dropped you…" She could hear the fury in Jasper's voice.

"He didn't."

"You're still engaged?" Jasper jerked his hand away from her arm. She missed it. And she liked that he would never even touch another man's woman, but it was clear that he wanted to touch her. Quite why was beyond her—did he really not see what a crippled wreck she was? But she wasn't going to be chasing him off anymore either.

"We never were. Different story for a different time."

Jasper looked thoughtful for a long moment, then slowly returned his hand to rest on her skin. This time, she was pretty sure that the gentle brushing of his fingertips was conscious.

"Once you got back, you were so…"

"I was so totally fucked up," Jana knew what she'd been.

"…down," Jasper concluded. "I wanted to help."

"Then what was with the silence thing?"

Jasper's fingers stopped and he looked down, his cowboy hat hiding his eyes.

"Jasper?" The silence stretched until she thought her head was going to crack.

"You already gave me your answer." He took his hand away and struggled to his feet. He turned for the door without looking at her.

"Jasper!"

He kept going.

"You turn around and set your ass right back in that chair. We're going to have this out now!" She'd sat up halfway, making the room spin. She flopped back down on the pillow and the pain bloomed to life—straight through the drugs. "Uh!" Jana could only grunt and squeeze her eyes shut while waiting for the spins and the pain to subside.

No hand returned to her arm, but after a long, whirling silence, she heard the slight scrape of the chair as Jasper settled back into it.

What was it that nobody wanted to tell her? Not Jasper. Not Maggie. Her brother had tried. Stacy had also tried—tried and failed. Something the doctor had told the others? But that didn't fit. She wiggled her toes and the fingers of her good hand to be sure. All accounted for.

She kept her eyes closed, the spins weren't quite gone yet.

"What did Stacy say to my brother?"

"She said that I loved you." Jasper said it flat out. No grumble or complaint. No sigh or hesitation.

Jana opened one eye and looked at him.

He was watching her from deep under the shadow of the cowboy hat's brim.

"And that meant that you'd never speak to me again?"

"I never spoke to you in the first place."

"Jasper!"

He groaned. "I was always scared shitless that you'd say 'no.' And *then* you *did."*

She had, hadn't she. "I was angry."

"So angry that you fell out of a parked helicopter and knocked yourself out cold." And Jasper's smile came out. She'd seen it with Curt or when he was with the other

41

guys. It had never been aimed at her before and it was a damned nice smile—even if he was teasing her. He *was* teasing her. That too was new.

"But—" Jana twitched her half-arm beneath his lingering hand. She was less than whole in so many ways.

"*That* doesn't have shit to do with who you are, Jana. I'm not that shallow. To my eyes, you're the most beautiful woman there is. If you think this changed that…" Jasper just shook his head sadly as he wrapped his fingers more tightly around the stub of her arm until he was holding it in a solid, intimate grip.

Jana had asked Curt once how he knew that Stacy was right for him. Even when pushed, his best answer had been that he "just knew."

Jana had never "just known" anything in her life.

Except maybe this one time she did.

Her phantom hand had gone quiet. No need to twitch her shoulder, click her hooks, or fool with her hair. Somehow, her missing hand was finally where it belonged —safe beneath Jasper's.

She slowly bent her half-arm toward herself. Jasper's grip held tight and he let the tension slowly draw him forward until his face was close by hers, under the shade of his cowboy hat.

He hesitated half an inch out, and she raised herself up just enough to kiss him. It wasn't some mild, gentle, hesitant kiss.

Jasper knew who she really was. Apparently better than she did. And he made it abundantly clear that he wanted her exactly as she was. His kiss built like a wave under her skin until it flushed with imagination of what would happen as soon as she was out of this bed and in another one.

She'd been kissed plenty before…well, before. She'd let

no man kiss her since the accident. Why would anyone want to? But amazingly one man did.

And maybe that one man was all she needed.

After he finally returned to the chair…

When her head stopped spinning from a hundred good reasons instead of one bad one…

While his hand still wrapped lightly about the stub of her arm more intimately than if they were holding hands…

Sleep began to slide over her. The emotional day, the concussion, everything. But there was one more question that had always bothered her.

"Jasper."

"Uh-huh."

"What's with the cowboy hat? You've been in Oregon since you were four."

"Six," but he chuckled. "Do you remember the first words you ever said to me?"

She tried to concentrate, but his kiss had left her in such a floaty, dreamy state that she couldn't seem to.

"It was on the day we moved in next door. First time I ever saw you, Jana."

"Sorry, I don't. Is that bad?"

"No. Not bad. It probably meant nothing to you. It changed my entire world."

"What was it?" Her eyes drifted shut, she couldn't fight off the sleep that overwhelmed her. It wasn't just the day and knocking herself out. It was also learning that this special man could love her just as she was— impossibly he saw her as whole. And now that he did, nothing else mattered. So many fears left behind. Without them she could see something she'd long forgotten—that the future was a place of hope. Even from that single kiss, some part of her *knew* that she'd walk beside this man for as long as they both should live. What girl didn't dream of that?

His lips brushed over hers once more, then he leaned in to whisper in her ear.

"You looked me square in the eye—you have such beautiful eyes, Jana—and you said, 'Nice hat.' I've worn one ever since just for you. I did all of it just for you."

WILDFIRE AT DAWN
(EXCERPT)

IF YOU LIKED THIS, YOU'LL LOVE THE SMOKEJUMPER NOVELS!

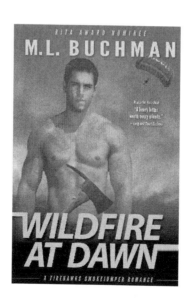

WILDFIRE AT DAWN

(EXCERPT)

*M*ount Hood Aviation's lead smokejumper Johnny Akbar Jepps rolled out of his lower bunk careful not to bang his head on the upper. Well, he tried to roll out, but every muscle fought him, making it more a crawl than a roll. He checked the clock on his phone. Late morning.

He'd slept twenty of the last twenty-four hours and his body felt as if he'd spent the entire time in one position. The coarse plank flooring had been worn smooth by thousands of feet hitting exactly this same spot year in and year out for decades. He managed to stand upright…then he felt it, his shoulders and legs screamed.

Oh, right.

The New Tillamook Burn. Just about the nastiest damn blaze he'd fought in a decade of jumping wildfires. Two hundred thousand acres—over three hundred square miles—of rugged Pacific Coast Range forest, poof! The worst forest fire in a decade for the Pacific Northwest, but they'd killed it off without a single fatality or losing a single town. There'd been a few bigger ones, out in the flatter

47

eastern part of Oregon state. But that much area—mostly on terrain too steep to climb even when it wasn't on fire—had been a horror.

Akbar opened the blackout curtain and winced against the summer brightness of blue sky and towering trees that lined the firefighter's camp. Tim was gone from the upper bunk, without kicking Akbar on his way out. He must have been as hazed out as Akbar felt.

He did a couple of side stretches and could feel every single minute of the eight straight days on the wildfire to contain the bastard, then the excruciating nine days more to convince it that it was dead enough to hand off to a Type II incident mop-up crew. Not since his beginning days on a hotshot crew had he spent seventeen days on a single fire.

And in all that time nothing more than catnaps in the acrid safety of the "black"—the burned-over section of a fire, black with char and stark with no hint of green foliage. The mop-up crews would be out there for weeks before it was dead past restarting, but at least it was truly done in. That fire wasn't merely contained; they'd killed it bad.

Yesterday morning, after demobilizing, his team of smokies had pitched into their bunks. No wonder he was so damned sore. His stretches worked out the worst of the kinks but he still must be looking like an old man stumbling about.

He looked down at the sheets. Damn it. They'd been fresh before he went to the fire, now he'd have to wash them again. He'd been too exhausted to shower before sleeping and they were all smeared with the dirt and soot that he could still feel caking his skin. Two-Tall Tim, his number two man and as tall as two of Akbar, kinda, wasn't in his bunk. His towel was missing from the hook.

Shower. Shower would be good. He grabbed his own

towel and headed down the dark, narrow hall to the far end of the bunk house. Every one of the dozen doors of his smoke teams were still closed, smokies still sacked out. A glance down another corridor and he could see that at least a couple of the Mount Hood Aviation helicopter crews were up, but most still had closed doors with no hint of light from open curtains sliding under them. All of MHA had gone above and beyond on this one.

"Hey, Tim." Sure enough, the tall Eurasian was in one of the shower stalls, propped up against the back wall letting the hot water stream over him.

"Akbar the Great lives," Two-Tall sounded half asleep.

"Mostly. Doghouse?" Akbar stripped down and hit the next stall. The old plywood dividers were flimsy with age and gray with too many showers. The Mount Hood Aviation firefighters' Hoodie One base camp had been a kids' summer camp for decades. Long since defunct, MHA had taken it over and converted the playfields into landing areas for their helicopters, and regraded the main road into a decent airstrip for the spotter and jump planes.

"Doghouse? Hell, yeah. I'm like ten thousand calories short." Two-Tall found some energy in his voice at the idea of a trip into town.

The Doghouse Inn was in the nearest town. Hood River lay about a half hour down the mountain and had exactly what they needed: smokejumper-sized portions and a very high ratio of awesomely fit young women come to windsurf the Columbia Gorge. The Gorge, which formed the Washington and Oregon border, provided a fantastically target-rich environment for a smokejumper too long in the woods.

"You're too tall to be short of anything," Akbar knew he was being a little slow to reply, but he'd only been awake for minutes.

"You're like a hundred thousand calories short of being even a halfway decent size," Tim was obviously recovering faster than he was.

"Just because my parents loved me instead of tying me to a rack every night ain't my problem, buddy."

He scrubbed and soaped and scrubbed some more until he felt mostly clean.

"I'm telling you, Two-Tall. Whoever invented the hot shower, that's the dude we should give the Nobel prize to."

"You say that every time."

"You arguing?"

He heard Tim give a satisfied groan as some muscle finally let go under the steamy hot water. "Not for a second."

Akbar stepped out and walked over to the line of sinks, smearing a hand back and forth to wipe the condensation from the sheet of stainless steel screwed to the wall. His hazy reflection still sported several smears of char.

"You so purdy, Akbar."

"Purdier than you, Two-Tall." He headed back into the shower to get the last of it.

"So not. You're jealous."

Akbar wasn't the least bit jealous. Yes, despite his lean height, Tim was handsome enough to sweep up any ladies he wanted.

But on his own, Akbar did pretty damn well himself. What he didn't have in height, he made up for with a proper smokejumper's muscled build. Mixed with his tan-dark Indian complexion, he did fine.

The real fun, of course, was when the two of them went cruising together. The women never knew what to make of the two of them side by side. The contrast kept them off balance enough to open even more doors.

He smiled as he toweled down. It also didn't hurt that

their opening answer to "what do you do" was "I jump out of planes to fight forest fires."

Worked every damn time. God he loved this job.

THE SMALL TOWN of Hood River, a winding half-an-hour down the mountain from the MHA base camp, was hopping. Mid-June, colleges letting out. Students and the younger set of professors high-tailing it to the Gorge. They packed the bars and breweries and sidewalk cafes. Suddenly every other car on the street had a windsurfing board tied on the roof.

The snooty rich folks were up at the historic Timberline Lodge on Mount Hood itself, not far in the other direction from MHA. Down here it was a younger, thrill seeker set and you could feel the energy.

There were other restaurants in town that might have better pickings, but the Doghouse Inn was MHA tradition and it was a good luck charm—no smokie in his right mind messed with that. This was the bar where all of the MHA crew hung out. It didn't look like much from the outside, just a worn old brick building beaten by the Gorge's violent weather. Aged before its time, which had been long ago.

But inside was awesome. A long wooden bar stretched down one side with a half-jillion microbrew taps and a small but well-stocked kitchen at the far end. The dark wood paneling, even on the ceiling, was barely visible beneath thousands of pictures of doghouses sent from patrons all over the world. Miniature dachshunds in ornately decorated shoeboxes, massive Newfoundlands in backyard mansions that could easily house hundreds of their smaller kin, and everything in between. A gigantic

Snoopy atop his doghouse in full Red Baron fighting gear dominated the far wall. Rumor said Shulz himself had been here two owners before and drawn it.

Tables were grouped close together, some for standing and drinking, others for sitting and eating.

"Amy, sweetheart!" Two-Tall called out as they entered the bar. The perky redhead came out from behind the bar to receive a hug from Tim. Akbar got one in turn, so he wasn't complaining. Cute as could be and about his height; her hugs were better than taking most women to bed. Of course, Gerald the cook and the bar's co-owner was big enough and strong enough to squish either Tim or Akbar if they got even a tiny step out of line with his wife. Gerald was one amazingly lucky man.

Akbar grabbed a Walking Man stout and turned to assess the crowd. A couple of the air jocks were in. Carly and Steve were at a little table for two in the corner, obviously not interested in anyone's company but each others. Damn, that had happened fast. New guy on the base swept up one of the most beautiful women on the planet. One of these days he'd have to ask Steve how he'd done that. Or maybe not. It looked like they were settling in for the long haul; the big "M" was so not his own first choice.

Carly was also one of the best FBANs in the business. Akbar was a good Fire Behavior Analyst, had to be or he wouldn't have made it to first stick—lead smokie of the whole MHA crew. But Carly was something else again. He'd always found the Flame Witch, as she was often called, daunting and a bit scary besides; she knew the fire better than it did itself. Steve had latched on to one seriously driven lady. More power to him.

The selection of female tourists was especially good today, but no other smokies in yet. They'd be in soon enough…most of them had groaned awake and said they were coming as he and Two-Tall kicked their hallway doors, but not until they'd been on their way out—he and Tim had first pick. Actually some of the smokies were coming, others had told them quite succinctly where they could go—but hey, jumping into fiery hell is what they did for a living anyway, so no big change there.

A couple of the chopper pilots had nailed down a big table right in the middle of the bustling seating area: Jeannie, Mickey, and Vern. Good "field of fire" in the immediate area.

He and Tim headed over, but Akbar managed to snag the chair closest to the really hot lady with down-her-back curling dark-auburn hair at the next table over—set just right to see her profile easily. Hard shot, sitting there with her parents, but damn she was amazing. And if that was her mom, it said the woman would be good looking for a long time to come.

Two-Tall grimaced at him and Akbar offered him a comfortable "beat out your ass" grin. But this one didn't feel like that. Maybe it was the whole parental thing. He sat back and kept his mouth shut.

He made sure that Two-Tall could see his interest. That made Tim honor bound to try and cut Akbar out of the running.

LAURA JENSON HAD SPOTTED them coming into the restaurant. Her dad was only moments behind.

"Those two are walking like they just climbed off their first-ever horseback ride."

She had to laugh, they did. So stiff and awkward they barely managed to move upright. They didn't look like first-time windsurfers, aching from the unexpected workout. They'd also walked in like they thought they were two gifts to god, which was even funnier. She turned away to avoid laughing in their faces. Guys who thought like that rarely appreciated getting a reality check.

Available at fine retailers everywhere.

ABOUT THE AUTHOR

M.L. Buchman started the first of, what is now over 50 novels and as many short stories, while flying from South Korea to ride his bicycle across the Australian Outback. Part of a solo around-the-world trip that ultimately launched his writing career.

All three of his military romantic suspense series—The Night Stalkers, Firehawks, and Delta Force—have had a title named "Top 10 Romance of the Year" by the American Library Association's *Booklist*. He also writes: contemporary romance, thrillers, and fantasy.

Past lives include: years as a project manager, rebuilding and single-handing a fifty-foot sailboat, both flying and jumping out of airplanes, and he has designed and built two houses. He is now making his living as a full-time writer on the Oregon Coast with his beloved wife and is constantly amazed at what you can do with a degree in Geophysics. You may keep up with his writing and receive a free book by subscribing to his newsletter at: www.mlbuchman.com

Join the conversation:
www.mlbuchman.com

Other works by M. L. Buchman:

SIGN UP FOR M. L. BUCHMAN'S
NEWSLETTER TODAY

and receive:
Release News
Free Short Stories
a Free Book

Do it today. Do it now.
http://free-book.mlbuchman.com

85727771R00040

Made in the USA
Lexington, KY
04 April 2018